Hooray! It's Book Day!

by Hilary Robinson

Illustrated by Stephen Holmes

FRANKLIN WATTS
LONDON • SYDNEY

About this book

Rhymes to Read are designed for children who are ready to start reading alone. They can also be used by an adult to share with a child.

The books provide excellent support for developing phonological awareness, helping the child to recognise sounds and sound-symbol relationships.
The poems are perfect to read aloud and the strong rhythms, rhymes and repetition will help build confidence and encourage reading and rereading for pleasure.

Reading tips for adults sharing the book with a child:
1. Make reading fun! Choose a time to read when you and the child are relaxed and have time to share the story.
2. Talk about the story before you start reading. Look at the cover and the blurb. What might the story be about? Why might the child like it?
3. Encourage the child to retell the story, using the pictures and rhymes to help. The puzzles at the back of the book provide a good starting point.
4. Give praise! Remember that small mistakes need not always be corrected.
5. For an extra activity, you could ask the child to make up some alternative rhymes for the story or their own brand new rhyme!

It was Book Day
at our school.
We dressed as
characters from books.

There were lots of
Red Riding Hoods
and lots of
Captain Hooks!

Alice came as Alice,
and Harry as a wizard.

Jack brought in
a beanstalk and
Jamie was a lizard.

10

We walked into
the classroom and
looked for Mr Platt.

Lying on his table was a tall and crooked hat.

We looked in every corner
and all around the room,

but all we found was
Wendy with a witch's
hat and broom.

There was an old umbrella, a toy ship and a rake,

a big red box,

a goldfish bowl,

a football and a cake.

We could not find
him anywhere. But
then a voice said, "Hey!

Children, what fun
we'll have while
your teacher is away!"

And in through the classroom door came a cat without his hat.

And everyone laughed

to see he was our teacher,

Mr Platt!

Puzzle 1

Put the pictures in the correct order and retell the story.

box
cake
ship
rake

leaf
wizard
wand
lizard

Find the rhyming words above.

Turn over for answers!

Answers

Puzzle 1

The correct order is: c, b, a.

Puzzle 2

The rhyming words are:

a. cake, rake

b. lizard, wizard

First published in 2011 by
Franklin Watts
338 Euston Road
London
NW1 3BH

Franklin Watts Australia
Level 17/207 Kent Street
Sydney
NSW 2000

Text © Hilary Robinson 2011
Illustration © Stephen Holmes 2011

The rights of Hilary Robinson to be
identified as the author and Stephen Holmes
as the illustrator of this Work have been
asserted in accordance with the Copyright,
Designs and Patents Act, 1988.

A CIP catalogue record for this book is
available from the British Library.

ISBN 978 1 4451 0297 9 (hbk)
ISBN 978 1 4451 0301 3 (pbk)

Series Editor: Melanie Palmer
Series Advisor: Catherine Glavina
Series Designer: Peter Scoulding

Printed in China

Franklin Watts is a division of Hachette Children's Books,
an Hachette UK company. www.hachette.co.uk